Amin loses his Way

SALARIYA
BH
BOOK HOUSE

Principle 3

Children's Rights

A min was five years old.
He was a dreamer: a playful and absent-minded little boy. He loved to gaze at the stars and never tired of watching the animals and their behaviour. He was very lucky because there was so much to interest him that he never got bored.

3

He belonged to a travelling tribe called the Taca-Taca. Whenever they moved on, they had to go as slow as a tortoise so that they would not lose sight of him, because Amin was very easily distracted. He liked to watch the giraffes munching the acacia leaves. His mother was always telling him: 'If you ever get lost, remember that your name is Amin and that Akida is your land. Don't forget.'

'Amin, please leave the zebras in peace, come on,' his mother told him, afraid that he would stray away from the path.
'You'll get lost one day!' the chief of the tribe told him, smiling.
And by chance, one day, those words came true.

Suddenly there was an almighty rainstorm, that took the tribe by surprise. The Taca-Taca had to move on faster than usual. Nobody noticed that Amin wasn't following, and the thunder drowned out his cries:
'Stop, please! Wait for me!'

Once the storm was over, Amin realised that he was lost, but he was sure that his tribe would find him sooner or later. He went off into the jungle in search of help. If he could only find a monkey with her baby, she was sure to help him and take care of him, too.

'Hello!' said Amin, greeting a family of monkeys. 'I thought you might be able to help me find my family.'

'Of course!' replied the monkeys. 'But you must climb up the tree first, because this is where we spend most of the day.'

The boy tried again and again, but each time he lost his balance and fell from the lowest branches onto his bottom.

'Apparently, the jungle is not your home,' suggested an old monkey. 'Follow the course of the river and ask the crocodiles.'

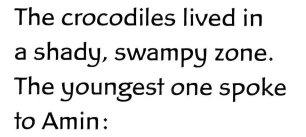

The crocodiles lived in
a shady, swampy zone.
The youngest one spoke
to Amin:
'If you want to stay with
us, you must be able to
swim very well, because
we spend most of the day
in the water.'

'I love getting my feet wet or running in the rain, but I couldn't bear to be in the water for so long.' The boy added: 'I would drown!'
'Then you won't feel at home with us and you can't call yourself a crocodile.'

The boy started running towards the grassland. There was a pride of snoozing lions. Amin liked sleeping a lot, too! So he asked them if he could be a lion and stay with them. 'As you wish,' replied a lioness. 'But when night falls, you must hunt a zebra for dinner.'

'A zebra?' he asked in surprise. 'I like watching them or making them run; I don't want to hurt them, though!'

'Perhaps *you* would like to be our dinner?' The youngest lions began to laugh. Amin ran away as fast as his legs would carry him.

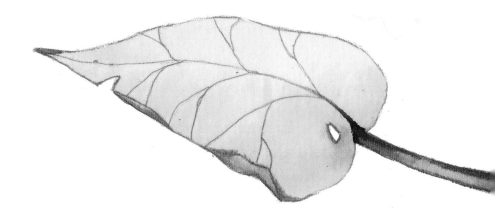

Tired and sad, he started thinking that
his name wasn't monkey, or crocodile,
or lion... It was Amin, a boy from Akida,
the land of the Akadinos. He had
to return and live with his own family.
Suddenly a voice said:
'You can stay with me, if you like...
I always like company.' It was a drowsy
porcupine under a shrub. 'Come
here and stay with me!'

The boy was so happy
to have finally found a
place to stay. Being next
to this little animal was
like being with his mother
or sister again. But as the
porcupine sat down
beside him, it stretched
out its spines.
'Ow! You pricked me!
How can we
live together?'

Amin gave up and left, not knowing what
to do or where to go. Being separated from his
tribe made him realise how important
it was for him to know who he was and where
he belonged; he just had to keep on searching.
It had been so long since anybody had called
him by his own name... Then:
'Aminnnnnnnnnnnn!' he heard in the distance.
'Where are you, Amin?'

'Here, I'm here!' he shouted as loudly as he could, when he saw his parents and the rest of the Taca-Taca. That night he would eat dinner, play and go to sleep just like any other Akida boy, beneath a roof, with his own people. Glad to be who he was, he yelled his name out loud...
How good it sounded!

Principle 3
of Children's Rights:

The child shall be entitled from his birth to a name and a nationality.

A person's name and nationality – or belonging to a country, which means the same thing – is a right that all boys and girls have, wherever they are. At the time of his or her birth, every newborn child is given a name to identify and distinguish that child from all other children.

Having a specific name, and belonging to a particular region of a country, helps to form an individual's personality. In the story, Amin was perfectly aware of his name and where he came from, but for a while he tried to become a part of the other 'nationalities' that are represented in the story by different animal families and their members. Logically, Amin doesn't fit in with any of them and cannot call himself by any other name, because he already belongs to a place called Akida and has a name that determines his identity, making him unique.

Children's Rights

Adopted by the General Assembly of the United Nations in Resolution 1386 (XIV) of 10 December 1959.

PREAMBLE

I. *Whereas* the peoples of the United Nations have, in the Charter, reaffirmed their faith in fundamental human rights and in the dignity and worth of the human person, and have determined to promote social progress and better standards of life in larger freedom,

II. *Whereas* the United Nations has, in the Universal Declaration of Human Rights, proclaimed that everyone is entitled to all the rights and freedoms set forth therein, without distinction of any kind, such as race, colour, sex, language, religion, political or other opinion, national or social origin, property, birth or other status,

III. *Whereas* the child, by reason of his physical and mental immaturity, needs special safeguards and care, including appropriate legal protection, before as well as after birth,

IV. *Whereas* the need for such special safeguards has been stated in the Geneva Declaration of the Rights of the Child of 1924, and recognised in the Universal Declaration of Human Rights and in the statutes of specialised agencies and international organisations concerned with the welfare of children,

V. *Whereas* mankind owes to the child the best it has to give,

VI. Now, therefore, *The General Assembly* proclaims this Declaration of the Rights of the Child to the end that he may have a happy childhood and enjoy for his own good and for the good of society the rights and freedoms herein set forth, and calls upon parents, upon men and women as individuals. And upon voluntary organisations, local authorities and national Governments to recognise these rights and strive for their observance by legislative and other measures progressively taken in accordance with the following principles:

Principle 1
The child shall enjoy all the rights set forth in this Declaration. Every child, without any exception whatsoever, shall be entitled to these rights, without distinction or discrimination on account of race, colour, sex, language, religion, political or other opinion, national or social origin, property, birth or other status, whether of himself or of his family.

Principle 2
The child shall enjoy special protection, and shall be given opportunities and facilities, by law and by other means, to enable him to develop physically, mentally, morally, spiritually and socially in a healthy and normal manner and in conditions of freedom and dignity. In the enactment of laws for this purpose, the best interests of the child shall be the paramount consideration.

Principle 3
The child shall be entitled from his birth to a name and a nationality.

Principle 4
The child shall enjoy the benefits of social security. He shall be entitled to grow and develop in health; to this end, special care and protection shall be provided both to him and to his mother, including adequate pre-natal and post-natal care.

The child shall have the right to adequate nutrition, housing, recreation and medical services.

Principle 5
The child who is physically, mentally or socially handicapped shall be given the special treatment, education and care required by his particular condition.

Principle 6
The child, for the full and harmonious development of his personality, needs love and understanding. He shall, wherever possible, grow up in the care and under the responsibility of his parents, and, in any case, in an atmosphere of affection and of moral and material security; a child of tender years shall not, save in exceptional circumstances, be separated from his mother. Society and the public authorities shall have the duty to extend particular care to children without a family and to those without adequate means of support. Payment of State and other assistance towards the maintenance of children of large families is desirable.

Principle 7
The child is entitled to receive education, which shall be free and compulsory, at least in the elementary stages. He shall be given an education which will promote his general culture, and enable him, on a basis of equal opportunity, to develop his abilities, his individual judgement, and his sense of moral and social responsibility, and to become a useful member of society.

The best interests of the child shall be the guiding principle of those responsible for his education and guidance; that responsibility lies in the first place with his parents.

The child shall have full opportunity for play and recreation, which should be directed to the same purposes as education; society and the public authorities shall endeavour to promote the enjoyment of this right.

Principle 8
The child shall in all circumstances be among the first to receive protection and relief.

Principle 9
The child shall be protected against all forms of neglect, cruelty and exploitation. He shall not be the subject of traffic, in any form.

The child shall not be admitted to employment before an appropriate minimum age; he shall in no case be caused or permitted to engage in any occupation or employment which would prejudice his health or education, or interfere with his physical, mental or moral development.

Principle 10
The child shall be protected from practices which may foster racial, religious and any other form of discrimination. He shall be brought up in a spirit of understanding, tolerance, friendship among peoples, peace and universal brotherhood, and in full consciousness that his energy and talents should be devoted to the service of his fellow men.

Visit our **new** online shop at
shop.salariya.com
for great offers, gift ideas, all our new
releases and free postage and packaging.

Published in Great Britain in MMXIII by
Book House, an imprint of
The Salariya Book Company Ltd
25 Marlborough Place, Brighton BN1 1UB
www.salariya.com
www.book-house.co.uk

1 3 5 7 9 8 6 4 2

A CIP catalogue record for this book is available from the British Library.

Printed and bound in China.

PB ISBN: 978-1-908973-28-3